AILY ✴ NEWS

SAFARI PARK SHOCK!
HOLE DISCOVERED IN FENCE!
ANIMALS MISSING

This morning, the keepers at the Safari Park were shocked to discover a large hole in the fence.

"I COULD BARELY BELIEVE MY EYES!" exclaimed head keeper Theodore Wilde.

Some animals are missing and the keepers have begun a search. "WE'RE BEARING UP UNDER THE STRAIN," said the team. Any public who may see al sights are ely to

The search will be ha "WE WILL GRIN BEAR IT," co

The Safari wi closed for hope

Happy ca said h carel w

For Vanny, Mark and Andrea,
and all their loved ones – A.S.

A TEMPLAR BOOK

First published in the UK in hardback in 2011 by Templar Publishing
This softback edition published in 2012 by Templar Publishing,
an imprint of The Templar Company Limited,
The Granary, North Street, Dorking, Surrey, RH4 1DN, UK
www.templarco.co.uk

First softback edition

ISBN 978-1-84877-452-0

Edited by Libby Hamilton

Printed in China

Silly Doggy!

by Adam Stower

templar publishing

One morning, Lily saw something wonderful in her garden.

It was big, brown and hairy.

It had four legs, a tail and a big, wet nose,

and Lily had ALWAYS wanted one…

Up close, he was quite big…

for a dog.

And a bit grumpy, too.

But Lily thought
he was lovely.

He just needed someone to look after him,
someone like Lily. So that's just what she did.

After a busy day together,

Lily and Doggy got home in time for tea.

Doggy was so much fun, Lily was sure that Mum

would let her keep him.

She didn't.

When Lily told her, Mum said Doggy would have a home
of his own, with people who would be missing him.

Lily supposed she was right. Probably.

So, to help Doggy's owners find him,
Lily made a poster…

FOUND!

One **very** silly doggy.

Colour: brown

Size: big and shaggy

Tail: short

Paws: ~~big~~ **very** big

Legs: yes

Smell:

wet blanket

and biscuits

He likes going to the park...

but he doesn't like walkies.

He's no good at tricks...

and he's terrible at playing fetch.

does what you tell him.

He can get sticky and mucky,
and he doesn't like bathtime.

But when he's washed, he looks very pretty.

His favourite thing is scratching.

My favourite thing is him.

Lily
x

When the poster was ready,

Lily and Doggy went out

to stick it up.

Secretly, Lily hoped no one would see it.

But, of course, someone did.

That night, even though she knew
he was happy back in his own home,
Lily felt sad that Doggy was gone.

But, the next morning,

she saw something

WONDERFUL

in the garden…

...ly ... some good news! And now ...at the Safari Park were ...ghted at the return of one of their favourite animals. "He's learned some new tricks," said the head keeper, "and will do anything for a tummy-rub!"

The public is warned that other ...mals from the Park are still at large.

PURR-FECT SCORE

Local girl Lily and 'Kitty' were the proud winners of this year's cat show. "What Kitty lacked in obedience, she made up for in teeth!" said the judge. Lily said she would use the prize – a season ticket for the Safari Park – to visit a very special friend.